FALSE
START

GRIDIRON

FALSE START

PAUL HOBLIN

darbycreek

MINNEAPOLIS

Darby Creek
A division of Lerner Publishing Group, Inc.
241 First Avenue North
Minneapolis, MN 55401 USA

For reading levels and more information, look up this title at
www.lernerbooks.com.

Cover and interior images: © pattern line/Shutterstock.com (scratched texture); © Eky Studio/Shutterstock.com (metal bolts); © Kriangsak Osvapoositkul/Shutterstock.com (rust texture); © ostill/Shutterstock.com (players); © EFKS/Shutterstock.com (stadium).

Main body text set in Janson Text LT Std 12/17.5.
Typeface provided by Adobe Systems.

Library of Congress Cataloging-in-Publication Data

Names: Hoblin, Paul, author.
Title: False start / Paul Hoblin.
Description: Minneapolis : Darby Creek, [2017] | Summary: Told in two voices, seniors Jeff and Scott compete on the high school football field but remain friendly until a scholarship and a girl come between them.
Identifiers: LCCN 2016047305 (print) | LCCN 2017006412 (ebook) | ISBN 9781512439793 (lb : alk. paper) | ISBN 9781512453515 (pb : alk. paper) | ISBN 9781512448689 (eb pdf)
Subjects: | CYAC: Interpersonal relations—Fiction. | Football—Fiction. | Competition (Psychology)—Fiction. | High schools—Fiction. | Schools—Fiction.
Classification: LCC PZ7.H653 Fal 2017 (print) | LCC PZ7.H653 (ebook) | DDC [Fic]—dc23

LC record available at https://lccn.loc.gov/2016047305

Manufactured in the United States of America
2-44633-25777-7/20/2017

Jeff

People understand why I'm mad at Scooter. They just don't understand why I'm *this* mad.

"We get it, Jeff," they say. "But is he really that bad? I mean, what did he do?"

So I tell them.

I tell them that he stole my starting spot on the football team. He stole my Division I scholarship. He stole Morgyn.

But I don't want their sympathy.

No. I need their help.

For getting revenge.

Chapter 2

Scooter

I know it sounds bad.

What was I thinking?

Let me just say this. Jeff's story isn't true.

Okay, it *is* true.

But it's not the *whole* story.

I, Scott Williams, a.k.a. Scooter, didn't really do all that Jeff thinks I did.

Jeff

None of this would have happened if Scooter hadn't moved to Small Valley for our senior year. Before he got here I was the starting running back. I was good too.

Actually, I was really good.

That's not bragging. When the all-conference list came out in the paper after my junior season, my name was on it: *Stoddard, Jeffrey. RB. Small Valley.*

There was no reason to think I wouldn't be all-conference as a senior too.

I'm a big guy. Big shoulders. Big legs. My shadow on the football field is the shape and size of a refrigerator.

I might not have breakaway speed, but I have quick feet for a guy my size. I also have soft hands for catching screen passes. Sometimes Coach Douglas puts me at tight end instead of running back so I can run routes. All you have to do is get the ball in my general direction, and I'll usually find a way to catch it.

Then Scooter showed up, and everything that *could* go wrong *did* go wrong.

Scooter

I sometimes wish I never moved to
Small Valley.

It's not like it was my choice.

My mom got a job here as a bank teller.
She'd been applying for months, and this was
the best job available. The problem, she said,
was that she didn't have a college degree.
That's why she wanted me to get more involved
in school; she read somewhere that kids who
were in school activities were more likely to get
college scholarships.

"Tell you what, Scott," she told me back
then, "if you promise to try your best at Small

Valley, I'll let you join the football team."

I'd wanted to play football since I was a kid, but my mom thought I was too little.

I *am* little. But so are a lot of running backs. My all-time favorite running back is Barry Sanders. He had already retired from the NFL by the time I was born, but his YouTube highlights are amazing. He was little too, but he juked and deked and ran circles around all the big guys trying to tackle him.

I'm a lot like Barry Sanders. Like me, he was really quick. Like me, he was really soft-spoken. (*Soft-spoken* is the word my mom uses to describe me. I think it just means really shy.)

I thought that maybe if I joined the football team, I wouldn't have to talk that much. Maybe I could just run the ball instead.

Then again, maybe Mom was right. Maybe I'd get crushed.

There was only one way to find out.

Chapter 5

Jeff

I still remember Scooter's first practice.

I'm pretty sure I'll never forget it.

I remember how all of us were on one knee, listening to Coach Douglas talk about our last game and his plan for practices for the week. I remember him stopping mid-sentence and saying, "I'm sorry . . . I completely forgot to introduce our new kid. Mr. Williams, stand up."

I looked where Coach was looking and waited for the player to jump to his feet and take off his helmet. He didn't do either.

"Stand up, son," Coach repeated.

This time, the player followed the command.

That's when I realized how tiny he was. It didn't help that he was hunching, his head drooped. It looked like the helmet was too big for him or something. It seemed to be weighing him down.

"Where are you from, Williams?" Coach asked.

The kid didn't respond. Or maybe I just couldn't hear him. It was hard to see whether his mouth was moving behind the face mask.

"What position do you play?" Coach asked. This time I heard him, but just barely.

"Running back," the kid mumbled.

That's when Coach turned to me. "Stoddard," he said. "Keep an eye on Williams, okay? Make sure he gets where he needs to be."

"Yes, sir," I said.

And I did. It was a total drag, but I did it anyway. The two of us went from drill to drill that day. I asked him where he played last year and he mumbled he hadn't, so I started breaking down terminology and our plays for him. The truth is, I felt sorry for him. I didn't know why he'd decided to go out for football this year, but then again it didn't matter. What mattered was that he was going to get crushed. It's not like I thought he'd be getting many handoffs. The running back position was already filled—by *me*. I'd worked hard last season and I didn't have any plans of stopping.

But a kid that small didn't need to be in a game for long to get hurt.

One carry would be enough.

"Williams!" Coach said toward the end of the practice. "Give Stoddard a breather."

I wanted to tell Coach that it was okay, I could keep going. But I knew better than to argue with him. I watched as the offense lined up without me—and with the tiny new kid standing a few yards behind our quarterback.

Scooter

As I stood there waiting for the play to start, I told myself to calm down.

C'mon, Scott, I thought. *This is your chance. Don't blow it.*

It's what I'd been thinking that whole first practice.

Like I said before, I've always been shy. But this was out of control. I'd hardly said a word the whole time—not even when the Coach or Jeff had asked me questions. I wanted so badly to impress them—to make them think that I wasn't just some runty kid with no football experience. Even though that's exactly what I was. It was like my brain and mouth had been disconnected. Most of the time I hadn't been able to think of anything to say. Even when I did come up with something, my mouth hadn't let me say it.

And now here I was, about to get my first handoff, and my brain had stopped working completely. Jeff had explained the difference between a dive and a veer, hadn't he? Which side did the coach say to run—right or left?

I couldn't remember.

"Hut!" the quarterback yelled.

Chapter 7

Jeff

It was like he was frozen there.

He wasn't moving an inch.

Our quarterback, Joey Mitchell, had taken the snap and turned to make the handoff. When he realized the running back wasn't there, he spun the other way. Still no running back.

By now the defense was breaking through the offensive line. Joey looked around frantically and finally found the running back in the exact same spot as where he'd started the play. Joey didn't have time to figure out what was going on. He had two options: get crunched by our defense or get rid of the ball.

He pitched the ball end over end to Scooter . . . who still wasn't moving.

I'm part of a lot of collisions—usually I'm the one who causes them. Bodies slamming into each other don't make me flinch.

But this was different.

Scooter was like a deer in headlights. He managed to catch the football somehow, but his feet were still stuck in the ground.

I closed my eyes and heard the collision.

When I opened my eyes, I saw bodies sprawled on the field, just as I expected.

What I didn't expect? The bodies weren't Scooter's. Two of our defensive linemen lifted their heads and looked at each other, dazed. Where had the little guy gone?

Honestly, it was like Scooter had disappeared.

Scooter

I'm not sure how I caught Joey's pitch. It was a matter of reflexes, I guess.

It wasn't something I thought about one way or the other.

Instincts. That's all it was.

Nothing else that happened was planned either.

Two guys were closing in on me, so I stutter-stepped. I half-spun. I ducked and lunged. Using my hand for balance, I stayed on my feet and scampered to my right. I planted a foot in the ground and cut back to the left and then again across the line of scrimmage.

One more cut and a stiff arm later and I was running free.

It wasn't until I got to the end zone that I had any idea of what I had just done. I turned back to the field and saw bodies strewn everywhere.

I did that, I thought. *This must be how Barry Sanders used to feel after a long run.*

Thinking of Sanders reminded me of how he acted after he scored touchdowns. No matter how incredible the run was, he didn't celebrate. He definitely didn't showboat. He just found a referee and hustled over to hand him the ball.

Since this was practice, there wasn't a referee. But there was Coach Douglas.

I ran the forty yards back to the line of scrimmage, head down, and handed the football to my new coach.

Jeff

A few minutes later, Coach Douglas blew his whistle and ended practice. As everyone shuffled off the field, Coach put his arm around me.

"Stoddard," he said. "Keep looking after the new kid, okay?"

"Look after him?" I asked.

"Help him learn the plays. Make sure he gets along okay at school. That sort of thing."

It's easy to blame Coach for a lot of what happened. All this time later, it seems like he was telling me to help Scooter take my starting job. But that's not really fair. At the time, I was still the all-conference starter, and Scooter was just a shy kid who had some speed. For all we knew, the incredible run he just made was a lucky chance. I don't think either one of us had any idea how good Scooter would end up being.

"What do you say, Stoddard?" Coach said. "Can you keep an eye on him?"

"Sure, Coach," I said.

I should have said no. I realize that now. If I'd said no, none of what happened next would have, well, happened next.

Scooter

No matter what Jeff and all his friends say about me now, I'm grateful for all of his help.

Without Jeff, I would never have learned the playbook or football fundamentals.

Without Jeff, I would never have felt like I was part of the team or the school.

Without Jeff, I would never have met Morgyn.

But I'm getting ahead of myself.

The first thing I would never have done is go to that party a few nights after our first practice.

Jeff

Yes, I agreed to look after Scooter. But that didn't mean I had to like it.

And I didn't. Not at first, anyway.

I invited him to a party and what did he do? Stared at the floor in silence, that's what. I kept trying to introduce him to all my friends. And not to brag, but I have a lot of friends. Small Valley High is football crazy, and I was one of the best players, so making friends has always been pretty easy for me. It should have been easy for Scooter too.

I even came up with a nickname for him. Yes, *that's* how he got the nickname.

"Hey, guys," I'd say. "I want you to meet my buddy. He's on the football team. Call him Scooter. Seriously, you should see the wheels on this guy."

Guys reached out to shake his hand or bump his fist. Girls smiled and waited for him to look up at them.

But he didn't reach his own hand out or lift his eyes an inch.

It was awkward and embarrassing.

Which is why I ditched him.

The dude was dead weight. Checking in on him? Sure, that I could handle. But babysitting him? No thanks.

That's what I told *myself* as I told *him*, "That's pretty much everyone. Have fun tonight, man."

Then I left him so I could have fun myself.

Scooter

I don't blame Jeff for stranding me at the party.

I was actually relieved when he left.

It meant I didn't have to meet anyone else. I don't know what's the matter with me, but for some reason, my mind goes totally blank when I try to come up with something to say to new people.

Anyway, when Jeff wandered off, I did too.

I ended up on the porch by myself. Coach had emailed me the playbook, and I scrolled through it on the phone. My only experience with playbooks was in videogames, which isn't really the same thing. I can't say that I totally understood what I was looking at, but it was better than being uncomfortable inside.

Still, it was cool when Jeff found me. No one's ever come looking for me when I've wandered off.

Jeff

At first I was angry. I go out of my way to bring this kid to a party and what does he do? He vanishes into thin air.

I was talking with some friends, having a good time. At some point, I stepped away from the conversation and looked around.

"What the . . . ?"

Then I was on the move.

"Have you seen Scooter?" I asked a few of the guys. They shook their heads.

The house was just one floor. It wasn't like there were a lot of places to go.

"The guy who walked in with me—is he

around here somewhere?" I asked someone else.

Maybe someone told me to check the porch. I can't remember. Then again, I might have figured it out myself.

"You're killing me, man," I told him as I stepped outside. "Coach asked me to keep an eye on you, but how am I supposed to do that when you sneak off like this?"

I regretted saying this as soon as it came out of my mouth. I only said it because I was so frustrated.

I was just about to apologize when Scooter said, "Coach asked you to keep an eye on me?"

He should have been offended by this news—I would have been—but it didn't sound like he was. In fact, I think he liked hearing that Coach was looking out for him.

"Why?" he asked.

It was the first thing he'd said to me in hours.

"I guess he thinks you have potential. That run today in practice was pretty impressive."

He thought about that and nodded. "I've always been better at avoiding people than interacting with them." He waved his phone at me. "Just trying to figure out the playbook. Maybe you could help me?"

I was pretty impressed. I bring a new guy to a party, and he wants to study the playbook? I guess his commitment to the team won me over a bit.

"I mean, you don't have to help me right now. You should go back to your party. But maybe—"

"I have a better idea," I interrupted. "Follow me."

As it turned out, this was not a good idea at all. In fact, it was the second terrible decision I'd made in a couple days.

Scooter

Jeff didn't tell me where we were going.

He just turned and walked back through the house.

It was the others who filled me in.

"Bet I know where you're going," one of the other guys on the team said to him.

"Pit stop at the girlfriend's, am I right?" our quarterback, Joey, said.

"Something like that," Jeff replied, pushing through the crowd with more determination than I'd seen from him since we left the field.

I'm not going to lie. I wasn't too excited about the idea of tagging along as Jeff made a stop at his girlfriend's. At best it sounded really awkward. We were in his car by now, moving through neighborhood streets, and I found myself hoping his friends were wrong. Maybe we weren't going to his girlfriend's. Maybe, instead, were going to the field to practice the plays I'd been trying to memorize. It was dark out, of course, but maybe Jeff knew how to turn on the lights. I imagined the two of us standing around the fifty yard line, running through one play after another.

We were definitely heading in that direction.

When we got there, though, Jeff didn't stop or even slow down.

We drove through neighborhood after neighborhood, toward the outskirts of town. We turned onto a dirt road, and then another. If he hated me then the way he hates me now, this would have been creepy. I would have been worried he was trying to find a quiet place to kill me and dump my body or something.

But he didn't hate me back then, so it never occurred to me to worry.

Still, I was curious.

"Are we really going to your girlfriend's?"

"Trust me. It's just what you need," he said.

More like just what you *need*, I thought.

"Couldn't you have just dropped me off at my place first?" I asked.

Jeff laughed. "It's not like that. Just trust me," he said again. "A little time in Morgyn's world would do us both some good."

Was he talking about his girlfriend? What did he mean her *world*?

A few minutes later we parked on the shoulder of the dirt road. Through some trees there was a small house with some lit-up windows.

I headed toward the house, but Jeff grabbed my shoulder. "This way," he said.

He guided me away from the front door, around the back of the house. It was darker back here, and there were more trees. Branches scratched against our arms as we worked our way deeper into the trees. A few feet later we came into a clearing. Ahead of us was a pond.

"I thought I'd find you here," Jeff said.

His voice sounded loud and echo-y over the water.

"Shhh," another voice said.

It was dark enough that I couldn't see the person very well until we were standing only a few feet away.

"Sorry," Jeff said. "Morgyn, meet Scooter. He's the new guy I told you about. Scooter, meet Morgyn. Don't try to talk to her about football, because she really won't hear it—not enough time. She always says she doesn't have enough time to get everything done."

"Shhhh," she said again.

Then she bent her legs and swung her arm. She stayed in a crouch, watching the black water.

"What are you doing?" I asked. It wasn't like me to blurt something out, but I was genuinely curious.

"She's skipping rocks," Jeff said.

"In the dark?" I asked. I wasn't sure who the question was for—Jeff or Morgyn.

"Who has time to skip rocks during the day?" she replied casually.

Jeff turned to me and gave me a look. "See what I mean?"

"Shhhhhh," she said.

Both Jeff and I listened. We waited for her to stop staring at the water.

"How many skips did you get this time?" Jeff asked.

"Eleven," she said. She was talking normally now instead of in a whisper.

"How do you know?" I asked.

But Morgyn didn't answer. By now my eyes had adjusted enough to the darkness to see what she was doing: feeling around for another rock to skip. When she found one to her liking, she straightened up.

"I listen," she said. "If you're totally quiet, you can hear the rock skimming off the water. It makes a pinging sound."

She threw the rock. The moon was bright enough that I saw the stone take its first big hop. Then it disappeared into the night.

I tried to listen for the pinging, but Jeff interrupted the silence: "How many that time?"

"Eight, I think," she said. "It's hard to hear when people are talking."

She was accusing Jeff, but she didn't seem to be too angry about it. This was an argument they'd clearly had before.

"Personally, I think she's making it all up. What do you think, Scooter? Could you hear anything?"

"I'm not sure," I admitted. "I want to try again."

Morgyn found another rock and sent it sailing toward the water. This time, I didn't even try to watch. I closed my eyes and concentrated.

Ping . . . ping . . . ping . . . ping . . . ping ping ping ping ping.

"Well?" Jeff asked again.

"Nine," we both said in unison.

Morgyn must have smiled because I could see her white teeth in the darkness.

"Ha! I *knew* you two would get along," Jeff said. "You guys could probably spend days together not saying a single word. If Morgyn had come to that party she probably would have ended up on the porch too."

Jeff picked up a rock and chucked it at the water. It crashed into the pond with a giant splash.

"Now that one I heard," he said.

We all laughed.

Of all the great things that happened over the next few months, many of them on the field, that moment was probably my favorite. Feeling comfortable. All of us laughing.

I didn't know then how complicated things would get.

Jeff

We didn't say much at first as I drove Scooter home.

"You were right," Scooter finally said.

"About what?"

I had the high beams on since we were driving on unlit dirt roads. Another car appeared, so I flipped the high beams off.

"About Morgyn," Scooter said. "She's really cool. Hanging out with her, it was like . . ."

His voice trailed off as he tried to find the right word.

"A break from your life?" I suggested.

He didn't answer, but out of the corner of my eye I saw him nod.

"That's how I feel too. Morgyn couldn't care less about my football career," I said. "I mean that in a good way. She's got her own priorities. Her parents are wilderness guides—they're gone a lot. She does a lot of fending for herself." Scooter still didn't say anything, but he was looking at me so I figured he was interested. "She goes to St. Amelia's, which is an all-girls, Catholic school. Sports really aren't a big deal there, and they definitely don't have their own team. She's never been to a pep rally in her life."

"How'd you meet her?" Scooter asked.

"Boy Scouts," I told him.

He lifted his eyebrows in surprise.

"She switched over from Girl Scouts. Said she'd rather learn how to build a fire than go door-to-door selling cookies."

"Is that allowed?" Scooter asked.

I turned onto the highway and felt the road go from bumpy to smooth.

"There was some special program. Not

everyone in the troop liked it at first, but eventually we realized she was a better Boy Scout than we were. Then she quit."

"Why?"

"I think she was sick of the group projects. I mean, she likes people—but she wants to do her own thing." I paused for a moment. "Kind of like how I need a break from our school sometimes. From football."

Scooter told me which roads to turn on to get to his apartment.

"Why do you need a break from football?" he asked.

I know I had brought it up, but the question caught me by surprise.

"I mean," he continued, "you're a star player. Everyone at the party clearly thought you were awesome. Why do you want a break from that?"

I pulled up to his apartment and put the car in park.

I'd just gotten done telling him all about Morgyn, but I wasn't ready to tell him about me. The answer to his question was that I needed a break from the pressure. Ever since I was in middle school I'd been training— running, hitting the weights—all so I could get a scholarship and keep playing football in college. But so far that scholarship hadn't come. And I was running out of time. Every carry felt like one of my last chances to impress college scouts who probably weren't even in the stands. I needed a break from football because I needed to figure out what to do if I couldn't keep playing.

But I didn't tell him any of this because I barely knew him. I didn't mind hanging with him outside of football. But on the field, we weren't friends or even just teammates. We were rivals.

It's not that I thought he was a bad guy—or that I even believed he was going to take my snaps. But I'm competitive. And I wasn't about to bare my soul to my competition.

"Long story," I told him instead. "See you at practice, man."

Scooter

We played Deerwood that Friday. I was nervous, but I couldn't figure out why. As far as I could tell, Coach Douglas had no plans to put me in the game. All week I'd taken part in drills, but that was it. Jeff got all the carries when we ran plays in practice.

For good reason too. The guy is a beast. And he's even more intense in actual games.

He spent the first half against Deerwood colliding into their defensive line, wearing them out. His legs never stopped churning. It always took more than one guy to take him down, and even then, he always fell forward—never backward.

That was Coach's plan all along: ram into the defensive line until it started to give in. That's how he laid it out for us at practice, and it's exactly what happened. We didn't score in the first quarter but we scored twice in the second—a bone-bruising six-yard touchdown run by Jeff and a thirty-two-yard field goal. In the third, we broke the game loose. It's not that we scored that many points; it's that Deerwood couldn't get our offense off the field. Jeff ran for first down after first down. He routinely got past the line and into the secondary, where he'd steamroll two or three defensive backs before they collectively brought him to the turf.

By midway through the fourth quarter, we'd had drives that lasted seven and ten minutes. We were up 24–3.

A few minutes later, Coach called my name: "Williams! Go in there and run out the clock!"

"I got this, Coach," Jeff said. "Let me finish what I started."

"You've done enough, Stoddard."

"They know we're running out the clock, Coach," Jeff said.

There was panic in his voice, and it took me a second to figure out why. If they knew we were running, Deerwood would put extra players in the box to clog the running lanes. Jeff was worried that I was going to get crushed.

Which made me mad. I mean, I knew his heart was in the right place, but I wasn't a baby. I didn't need his protection. How pathetic did he think I was?

"Are you up for it, Williams?" Coach asked.

The true answer was that I wasn't sure. But the true answer wasn't the right answer. If I wanted to play in the future, I knew what I had to say. I had to prove to Jeff—and even myself—that I could do it.

"Absolutely, Coach."

Jeff

I understood what Coach was doing. He was taking me out of the game to make sure I was still healthy for next week's game.

I understood the decision, but that doesn't mean I had to like it. Adrenaline was flooding my body, so any pain I'd feel the next day was a non-issue right then.

But I also thought it was cruel to send Scooter out there. It wasn't just Deerwood; everyone in the stadium knew that we were running the ball. With a guy Scooter's size, it seemed to me that we should only be putting him in on plays where the defense thought we might pass. That way, they wouldn't have so many players looking to pounce on him.

It was better to have our QB sacked by whoever got to him first than to have eight guys pile on top of Scooter. At least Joey was a big enough guy to be able to take a hit.

I give Scooter credit though. It took courage for him to take that handoff.

Either that or it took stupidity.

Once he had the ball, Scooter managed to squirm through a crack in the offensive line.

Then, a mass of Deerwood bodies closed in on Scooter.

But Scooter emerged on the other side of the pile. To this day I don't understand how he did it. The entire defensive line had thrown themselves at him in one giant clump of players. It was pure chaos, with limbs flying everywhere and Scooter buried somewhere in the middle, but then out of nowhere Scooter emerged, somehow unscathed. It was surreal—almost like an old cartoon where the hero emerges from the middle of a giant fight, leaving the bad guys to continue beating each other up. Scooter ran away from the pileup of other players and scampered down the sideline.

There were two Deerwood players left to beat—the free and strong safety—but he had nowhere left to run. The sideline cut off any escape route except going out of bounds. And that's exactly what I expected him to do. Sure, running out of bounds would stop the clock, which we didn't want to do. But honestly, Scooter had done more than enough. This was supposed to be a one-yard run. Instead, he'd turned it into a thirty-eight yarder. The next thing to do was step out of bounds and run another play.

But that's not what Scooter did. He planted his foot and turned back into the field. The two safeties arrived at the same time, and they did indeed bring him down—but somehow he wriggled his body so that neither defender hit him very hard.

Scooter

When I got up and went back to the huddle for one more play (a QB kneel), I was surprised by all the cheering.

The truth? I was disappointed in myself. I'd been trying to figure out a way to get into the end zone, but I'd stupidly let myself get pinned to the sideline.

That's not how anyone else saw it though. In the days after the game, teammates and other students told me my run was the highlight of the game. They said I'd pulled a Houdini. I still don't see what the big deal is. I made a few stutter steps and faked a few guys out. What's so magical about that?

Every time I tried to shrug these people off though, they said things like "Oh, and he's modest too!"

That was maybe the weirdest part. All my life, my shyness had been a bad thing. My mom and other teachers had tried to get me "out of my shell." Now it was just me being humble.

Apparently, in Small Valley one run was enough to make me a star.

Don't get me wrong. I was glad to prove myself. Jeff had clearly thought I'd get crushed. I think even Coach didn't trust that I would be able to pull off another great run.

But the hype *was* way over the top. It was Jeff who had been the star of the game. How could no one see that?

By the middle of the week, it seemed like everybody was insisting that there was some kind of huge running back controversy. People were debating the pros and cons of big vs. small running backs. And then on Thursday, Coach Douglas called the two of us into his office after practice.

"Stoddard, you're not going to lose your starting job," he said.

Which made sense to me.

"You're going to share it," he said.

Jeff

"Coach?" I was stunned.

This had to be a joke. How could Coach Douglas honestly consider demoting me because of one run?

"Take it easy, Stoddard," Coach said. "This is a good thing—for both of you."

My face must have looked skeptical because Coach continued, "Just hear me out. Ever heard of Mike Alstott and Warrick Dunn?"

I knew who they were, but I didn't answer. Scooter didn't either. I think we were both trying to figure out where this was going.

"They were both running backs for the Tampa Bay Buccaneers in the 1990s. They went by the nicknames Thunder and Lightning. Alstott was a power back. Dunn was a speedster. Do you see where I'm going with this?"

Again we didn't answer. He didn't seem to expect us to.

"You're going to share the carries, boys. Stoddard, you're going to hit the defensive line like a sledgehammer to a plaster wall. Williams, you're going to shoot past their crumbling defense and run circles around the secondary. How does that sound to you?"

We still didn't answer.

Coach was beaming. I'd never seen him look so happy. "Thunder and Lightning, boys. Thunder," he paused for dramatic effect, "and lightning."

Scooter

"This is crazy, right?" I asked Jeff.

It was a real question. I honestly didn't know for sure if Coach had lost it.

We were in the locker room, sitting on the bench by our lockers.

He grunted. "You can say that again."

"How do you think it's going to work?" I asked. "Will we switch off every series, or every quarter, or . . . ?"

"I don't know, Scooter. I'm still trying to figure out why Coach thought I'd be happy sharing carries."

Jeff stood up. "I gotta get out of here."

"Where you going?" I asked.

"Someplace where I don't have to think about football."

I was pretty sure I knew where that was. I almost asked if I could go with him, which I know sounds crazy. When he said he wanted to get away from football, he was saying he wanted to get away from me—or at least the situation I had caused.

But I hadn't stopped thinking about Morgyn since the other night. She was a little weird, but in a good way. Here I was hoping Jeff would say everything was fine, that he'd be happy to share carries with me—but it was more complicated than that. All of the politics and pride wasn't what I wanted. I liked football because it was the one place where I didn't have to try to talk to people and explain myself. I didn't even have to think. But Morgyn seemed to always do that. She did what she wanted to do without needing to give an explanation.

This is what I was thinking as Jeff left the locker room.

Jeff

Scooter should have spoken up. It's as simple as that. He sat there in that meeting and let Coach give him my carries, and he didn't say anything until we left the office.

Was this expecting too much? Maybe. But I was mad.

Not just at Scooter but at the whole situation.

I'd done everything right. I'd looked after Scooter, just like Coach asked. I'd spent two seasons blasting my body through the teeth of the defense, just like Coach asked. But that's where I drew the line. If Coach had asked me to give up my carries, I would have said no way.

Unfortunately, he didn't ask. He announced.

These were the thoughts that were rattling around my head as I arrived at Morgyn's.

I found her out back.

She was chopping wood, getting ready for her annual fall bonfire. I went to the equipment shed under the deck and helped myself to work gloves and an ax.

Morgyn and I didn't talk. We chopped. This is how it's always been with us. Morgyn respects my head space. I never have to worry about doing or saying the wrong thing when I'm around her.

We took turns. When she was the one swinging the ax, I gathered loose chunks of wood and piled them on a sled. Once the sled was full, one of us would drag it to the wood pile about thirty yards away.

When it was my turn to chop, I brought the ax down with all the power I could muster. It felt good, clenching and then releasing the muscles in my shoulders, back, and legs. I wasn't just chopping the wood. I was taking my anger out on it.

"Something on your mind?" Morgyn asked.

"Is it that obvious?" I responded.

"I'm pretty sure the wood is actually cowering."

She asked if I wanted to talk about it.

"Not really," I said.

Which was good enough for her.

"My turn," she said, picking up her ax.

Chapter 22

Scooter

The next day we played South Hill.

It was an away game, and the South Hill fans were *crazy*.

Crazy about football. Crazy about their team. And mostly, crazy about their team's defense.

"DE-FENSE!" they shouted over and over. "DE-FENSE!"

Throughout the first half, they had a lot of reasons to chant.

The main reason was me.

Maybe they heard about my long run the week before. Whenever I got the ball, it looked like their entire team was running after me. I did everything I could think of to gain some yards. I'd juke one guy and fake out someone else, only to have four other guys breathing down my neck. Mostly, I ran side to side along the line of scrimmage, trying but failing to find a hole to cut into. By the end of the half, I must have run for a hundred yards. But all of it was sideways.

"DE-FENSE! DE-FENSE!"

Jeff had more success. He barreled into the heart of the defense. I don't know how many yards he ended the half with—Thirty-five? Forty? But they were all helpful.

Thanks to Jeff, we were able to move the chains. By getting first downs, we stayed on the field—even if we didn't score many points.

As we entered the locker room at the half, we were down 10–3.

But for some reason, Coach didn't seem too concerned.

"Keep doing what you're doing, boys," he told Jeff and me. He was fired up. "That defense has gotta be sore and tired. They can't last forever—not when they're overcommitting like that. If we get by that wall, there's no one left to beat." He turned to Jeff, grabbed his face mask. "Stoddard, keep blasting away at them, you hear?"

Chapter 23

Jeff

"I hear you loud and clear, Coach," I said with a smile.

At the start of the second half Coach sent me back on the field.

A few moments later, Joey, our QB, handed me the ball. I didn't bother waiting for a hole to open up. I wanted to make the hole myself.

Leading with my shoulder, I launched myself forward. The sound of my body smashing into other bodies filled the ear holes of my helmet. My body stiffened, shocked by the collision—but only briefly. In the blink of an eye, my feet were on the ground again. I dug my cleats into the field, pushing, straining, moving forward. More South Hill players joined in. One of them grabbed me by the ankles, stopping my momentum and bringing me to the ground.

All in all it was a six-yard run. But it was more than that.

They were softening, giving in. I could feel it.

They were weakening.

Coach had been right. Throughout the first half it had felt like I was running into a brick wall. Now that wall was eroding.

As for me? I was getting stronger.

On the next play I gained eight more yards. Then four. Then eleven.

I almost felt bad for them. They didn't stand a chance against me this half.

"Stoddard!" Coach yelled. "Take a breather!"

Are you kidding me?!

Scooter

Thunder and Lightning.

Jeff had provided the thunder. Now it was my job to bring the lightning.

If I could.

When I got the ball, I hesitated. For the first time, there was a clear running lane in front of me. I darted through it and saw that Coach was right. They had overcommitted— blitzed almost everyone.

There was a cornerback to my left, but he was still fifteen yards away.

The South Hill free safety was the only real concern. He was a few yards away, but he was on his heels.

Big mistake.

In the YouTube highlights, even NFL players used to make this mistake against Barry Sanders. Once Sanders got in the open field, the only way you had a chance against him was to be decisive. To get where he was cutting next, and hopefully guess correctly.

Don't get me wrong. I'm not saying I'm Barry Sanders—just that the free safety was making the same mistake as those guys in the clips. He was waiting for me to make a move. He was bargaining that he'd be able to react to that move in time to stop me from breaking free.

It was a bad bargain.

I faked with my head and hips to the left, then cut to the right.

His body mirrored mine, or tried to. Instead, he just fell down.

One move. That's all it took. Two, if you count the hip shimmy.

The next thing I knew, I was in the end zone. And the South Hill fans had stopped chanting. And all my teammates were piling around.

Except Jeff.

He stood there on the sideline, head down, refusing to look up.

Jeff

I created the hole Scooter ran through. Me.

We won the game, 17–10.

So why, in that moment, did it feel like I had lost?

Scooter

I get it. Jeff was furious. And he had good reasons.

Because here's the thing about thunder and lightning.

You only *see* the lightning.

Fans don't pay attention to the four-yard run, even if it set up the forty-yard run.

That next week Coach tried to explain to the local reporters how well Jeff had played. But they didn't want to hear about it.

All my life I've been shy, but that week I forced myself to speak up. "The real hero of the game was Jeff," I said. "When you're done talking to me, you should talk to Jeff."

Jeff, Jeff, Jeff. He's all I talked about.

All they heard, though, was a kid trying to say all the right things.

We all like it when the star player says the right things. But we find it boring too. We give them credit for spouting clichés. But we also treat their words as a waste of time.

By mid-week, I'd given up and gone quiet again.

Honestly, I felt bad for Jeff, but what's the point of speaking up if no one's listening?

Jeff

Sure, a few people asked me questions about the game. But it never took them long to get to what they really wanted to talk about: Scooter.

What's he really like?

Does his soft-spoken presence have a calming influence on the locker room?

Coach told me over and over again that I was just as important as Scooter. He pointed out that I was making Scooter's life easier every time I touched the ball. And I knew he was right.

But nobody else seemed to.

Based on all the questions I was getting,

people seemed to think that having Scooter around was making *my* life better. And I didn't see how that could possibly be true.

Thunder and Lightning. How dumb.

Look, I was trying. I was doing my best. But I didn't know how much longer I could keep it up.

Don't any of you know ANYTHING about football? I wanted to ask.

Has a single one of you noticed that I've had two consecutive one-hundred-yard rushing games?

Then, two days before our next game, Coach called Scooter and me into his office. Someone, it turned out, *had* taken notice of me.

And that someone was a college scout.

Scooter

Coach Douglas was pleased but trying not to show it. For my benefit, I think.

"I told him we had another running back named Williams who was raw but talented," Coach assured me. "I said you weren't ready to play college football yet, but that they should consider letting you walk on. You had that much upside."

"Thanks, Coach," I said.

Coach had just learned that a scout from Huntington College was interested in Jeff. He'd be in the stands on Friday.

Coach had called both of us into the office

to announce the good news. Once he told us, though, I think he felt bad for dragging me in there.

But I didn't feel bad. I'd only been playing for a month. I definitely didn't expect scouts to come flocking.

"Stoddard, you've been unusually quiet," Coach said. "What's on your mind, son?"

"Just surprised, Coach," he said. "I thought that ship had sailed. And then I spent all week hearing about how great Scooter is. No offense, Scooter."

No offense was taken. He hadn't really been saying much to me all week, so it was cool to hear him concerned about my feelings.

"I'm just . . . surprised," he repeated.

I was happy for him. That's the truth.

After all, this was a dream come true for him.

Or at least it seemed that way.

Jeff

As furious as I am now, I felt the opposite when Coach told me about the scout. I was on top of the world during the next game.

I'd been working nonstop since I was in middle school, doing everything I could to get bigger, stronger, faster—*better*. Football is a physical and even violent game. So I made myself into a human battering ram who could take any and all abuse.

My teammates and Coach—even my school—cheered me on.

But the rest of the world?

Not so much.

I know that sounds dramatic, but it's how I felt. I *knew* I could play college football, but for some reason, colleges didn't seem to agree.

Football may be violent. But people don't seem to pay as much attention to the ones who take and deliver this violence. They're much more interested in the ones who run away from it.

That's how it felt, anyway, until I learned about the scout.

It turned out that someone *was* paying attention to me.

And maybe it makes me selfish to care about this. Maybe it makes me vain to want that kind of attention. But when you've gotten and given as many bruises as I have, at some point you have to ask yourself whether it's worth it.

For the first time all season, it seemed like it was.

Scooter

That Friday Jeff was unstoppable.

Every time it looked like he'd been tackled, he'd add another three yards to the run by dragging whoever was trying to bring him down.

We were playing Woodgrove. They were small—individually and as a team. We had over sixty guys on our roster; they had twenty.

It would have taken all twenty to stop Jeff that day.

Coach abandoned his "Thunder and Lighting" plan and stuck with the thunder—mostly, I think, to give the Huntington scout a good look at Jeff.

We spent the first half marching down the field in seven- to ten-yard chunks.

We scored four touchdowns on four long drives. Instead of kicking extra points, Coach opted to give the ball to Jeff for the two-point conversion. He bullied his way into the end zone each time.

The second half was more of the same.

The nice thing about running so much is that the clock doesn't stop like it does for an incomplete pass. That means the game was mercifully short for Woodgrove.

In the fourth quarter Jeff was taken out of the game. He got a loud ovation from our home crowd.

"Williams," Coach said, grabbing my face mask, "let's not run up the score, okay?"

"You want me to let them tackle me, Coach?" I asked.

"I didn't say that. I just said don't get in the end zone. As for getting tackled, the longer you can avoid that, the fewer plays we need to run." To my surprise, he smiled. "Have you ever played old football video games, Williams?"

"How old, Coach?"

"Old," he said. "In the oldest video games, the good players are so much faster than the bad ones that they can literally run circles around them. Think you can do that, Williams?"

Now I was the one smiling. "I'll try, Coach."

When Joey handed me the ball I ran toward the sideline instead of the line. Then I turned back and ran the other way. I cut and spun; I turned up the field, but then circled back. Woodgrove chased me this way and that. Finally, they brought me down—two yards behind the line of scrimmage.

I looked at Coach. He nodded his approval, so I did it again on the next play. I zig-zagged, pumped my legs, and changed course. This time I was brought down after gaining four yards but staying upright for thirty-two seconds.

The crowd loved it; they laughed and cheered. Coach, on the other hand, changed his mind. He was probably worried Woodgrove would feel like we were showing them up.

I was glad he changed his mind. Frankly, I was exhausted.

Coach ordered Joey to take two straight knees. Woodgrove got the ball back with less than a minute to go.

I stood on the sidelines next to Jeff. Even through his face mask I could see he was beaming. I was pretty happy too. Jeff had done really well. And it had been fun to see how long I could stay upright with an entire team chasing me.

Overall, a win-win situation. Or so I thought.

Chapter 31

Jeff

I watched the clock on the scoreboard tick down to zero.

Don't turn around, I kept telling myself.

I wanted to show the scout that I was a team player, that I was more focused on my team than him. I clapped my hands and shouted encouragement. When guys ran back to the sideline, I slapped them on their helmets or shoulder pads.

I'm not going to lie though. Every fiber of my being wanted to turn around and find the scout sitting somewhere in the stands.

What if I never *did* find him? How did this

work? Would he call me or something?

Luckily, I didn't have to find him. He found me.

There was no time left on the clock when I heard someone say, "Jeffrey? Jeffrey Stoddard?"

I turned and took off my helmet.

He was on the track that surrounded our field. A small guy, decked out in red and blue. In other words, Huntington College colors.

"Can I have a word?" he asked.

You can have as many words as you want, I thought.

"That was one heck of a performance, Jeffrey. You're quite the player. A high school star."

"Thank you, sir," I said.

Now that he was standing next to me, I saw just how short he was. Even shorter than Scooter, who was standing on my other side.

"No need to call me sir," the man said. "Name's Eric. Eric Musselman. I saw your recent box scores and contacted your coach. He told me I wouldn't regret making the trip to see the game. He was right."

"Thank you, sir," I said again. "I mean, Eric. I mean, Mr. Musselman."

"Eric's fine," he said.

He was staring intently at me. I remember that. At the time I thought it was a good sign. I thought it meant he truly was taking notice of me. Now I wonder if he was counting down the seconds to talk with Scooter.

"I'd like you to visit the campus sometime next week. Would that work for you?"

"I'm sure it would . . . Eric."

"Great. Bring your teammate too." This is when he first turned to look at Scooter. "Scott Williams, is it?" He looked at his clipboard to double check, then back up at Scooter. "We're always looking for walk-ons."

Scooter did what he usually does. He dropped his head and went mute. I couldn't help but feel bad for him. As much as I hated all that had happened to me since he came to town, it wasn't necessarily his fault. In any case, it wasn't worth letting him risk a spot to play on a college team.

So rather than let him sabotage his own

future, I put in a good word.

"He goes by Scooter, Eric," I explained. "And he's got some serious wheels."

"I saw that," the scout said. "We just need to get you to run in the right direction, son, and we might really have something there."

He cracked a smile to let us know he was kidding.

I elbowed Scooter until he returned the smile.

Eric turned to me. "I'll tell the coaching staff to expect you two boys soon."

"You got it, sir—er, Eric."

Scooter

I didn't want to go.

Nobody would believe me if I said it out loud, least of all Jeff.

But let the record show: I, Scott "Scooter" Williams, didn't want to visit Huntington College.

Because what was the point?

There was no way I was going to walk on to their football team. If you walk on, you don't have a scholarship. And without a scholarship, I couldn't afford to go to college.

The only reason I *did* go was to make my mom happy. She wanted me to attend college so badly that, frankly, she was in serious denial. She couldn't bear to face the truth. We didn't have the money.

Oh, and there's another reason I went: to make Jeff happy.

Once again, I don't expect anyone to believe me, but it's true. Jeff was so excited by the visit and he really stood up for me. I couldn't say no. Not when things were finally smoothing out between the two of us.

So that's how I ended up riding with Jeff to Huntington College the next week.

"Thunder and Lightning, man," he kept saying on the car ride. All of the sudden, he loved this nickname. "You and me, college bound. Maybe we'll be roommates."

I nodded.

No, we won't, I thought.

As it turned out, I was right—but for the wrong reason.

Jeff

That was the worst day of my life.

I just didn't know it yet.

At the time, I thought it was the best day of my life.

Scooter and I arrived on campus and then asked a student how to find the athletics building. As we walked across the campus I couldn't help but feeling like I already belonged. I wondered which dorm I would live in and could almost picture myself studying in the library. With each step I grew more comfortable on the campus.

When we got to the athletics building we approached the front desk.

"I'm Jeff Stoddard," I said. "I think they're expecting me. I mean, us," I said, catching myself. "This is Scooter—Scott Williams. He was invited too."

The guy at the front desk picked up a phone, punched in a number, and repeated our names.

"Take a seat," he said. "They'll be out to see you soon."

Scooter and I sat down in a couple of rubbery chairs. He was doing that head-drooping thing he always does in social situations. "Chin up, dude," I told him. "They asked you to come, remember? Show them you know you belong."

A door opened and two guys walked out. They were maybe in their mid-thirties and introduced themselves as assistant coaches.

"How'd you like a tour of the facilities?" one of them asked.

"Sounds great," I said. Both Scooter and I stood up.

"We'd like to just take you on the first leg of the tour, Jeff," the other coach said. "Easier to talk that way. We'll swing by and pick up Scooter in a few minutes."

I saw Scooter's head droop again.

"Hey," I mouthed, punching his shoulder. "Chin up."

Chapter 34

Scooter

I watched Jeff and the coaches walk away and I wondered, again, *Why am I here?*

I was just sitting down when the door opened again. It was the same door the coaches had come out of a few minutes ago.

An older man peered around the door.

"Scott Williams?" he said.

I was surprised he knew my name. I would have been surprised if *anyone* here knew my name. I'd never met any walk-ons before, but I doubted many of them were on a first-name basis before the school year even started.

"Could I have a word with you?" the man asked.

"I'm actually waiting for my buddy," I mumbled.

I don't think he could hear me because he said, "Eric said you were shy."

Eric? Who was Eric?

Then I remembered: the scout.

"It'll just take a few minutes, Scott," he said. "They call you Scooter, right?"

Now he knew my nickname?

"You'll be sitting back in that chair by the time Jeff gets back," the man said. "That work for you?"

Jeff

The coaches took me to the weight room. I thought maybe the team would be working out there, but it was empty.

Maybe that's just something that happens in movies, I thought.

They asked me if there was anything else in particular I wanted to see.

"The stadium?" I said.

"Sure, kid," one of them replied.

I was a little bummed that I had to ask. In the days leading up to this visit, I'd imagined walking through a tunnel into the stadium on my first game day. There would be cheerleaders. JEFF STODDARD would flash on the jumbotron. An announcer would introduce me over the loudspeaker, his voice echoing. Instead, we walked out onto the quiet field. Still, I felt at home there.

Scooter

"**P**lease sit down, Scooter," the old man said.

I did, and watched him do the same.

We were in an office. A *big* office. The walls were covered in pennants and plaques.

"Do you know who I am?" the man asked.

I shook my head.

"My name's Coach Grand. That's not bragging. It's my name."

He winked at me. I wondered how many times he'd made that joke over the last few decades.

"I'm the head coach here at Huntington," he said.

"What's going on?" I blurted out. I was too confused and curious to keep my mouth shut any longer.

"I thought you were supposed to be shy," Coach Grand said. "Maybe there's more to you than meets the eye."

I wasn't sure whether this was a compliment or not. But I *was* sure he hadn't answered my question.

"What am I doing here?" I asked.

He leaned back in his chair. "We're looking for speed on offense, Scooter. Eric tells me you've got the potential to be quite the little scat back."

"I can't, Coach. I should have told someone before I got here, but I can't afford to come here. It was really nice of Eric to put in a good word for me but—"

"You wouldn't have to pay, Scooter," Coach interrupted. "I'm talking about a scholarship."

I'm not going to say I wasn't excited. Of course I was. I was on the verge of literally jumping for joy. But I also didn't understand.

"Why?" I asked.

He chuckled. "In all my years coaching, that's the first time a player has ever responded to a scholarship offer by questioning my decision."

"I just mean . . ." I forced myself to breathe, clear my head, get my thoughts straight. "Based on what? I barely even played last week."

"Eric said you played enough to put on a dazzling display. He said you had the whole team chasing after you. He said you've got elite shiftiness and speed. And he's not someone who throws words like that around. If he says you're elite, I believe him."

I wracked my brain trying to come up with more questions to ask. But I was too excited to think of any.

"I can't wait to tell Jeff. He kept talking about how we could go to college together; we've got this nickname, Thunder and Lightning, it's kind of stupid but—"

"Just to be clear," Coach interrupted, "I'm offering *you* a scholarship, not Jeff."

"I don't understand."

"I only have one scholarship left, Scooter, and if you want it, it has your name on it."

"But Jeff was invited to visit, not me."

"I wish Eric hadn't handled it that way. I know it makes this awkward. But frankly, he wasn't expecting to find someone like you—and in the last few minutes of the game, no less. He wasn't sure how to get you here, what with your so-called shyness, and he knew he didn't want to leave without making sure you'd be at our campus, one way or another. So he got Jeff to bring you along on his visit."

I thought about Jeff touring the facilities. I thought about how happy he must be.

"Thanks, but . . ." I took a deep breath and tried to wrap my head around what I was about to say. "Give the scholarship to Jeff. He's earned it."

"You don't understand, Scooter. I'm not offering it to Jeff. Eric tells me he's a truly solid high school ballplayer. Strong. Tough. Yes, solid's the word. But I'm not looking for solid. I'm looking for fast. I'm looking for game-changing. I'm looking for you, Scooter." Coach

Grand swayed his head back and forth, as though he were weighing his options. "Or for someone like you, if you don't accept my offer."

He checked his watch. "We better get you back in that chair where I found you." Standing up, he moved to the door and held it open for me. "I don't expect you to decide today. But you do need to decide quickly. Eric and my other scouts are traveling all over the country, trying to find someone just like you."

He ushered me out the door and began to close it.

"Coach?" I said. "What am I supposed to tell Jeff?"

"It's up to you," he said. "But if it were me? I wouldn't tell him anything—at least not yet. Not if you still want a ride home."

Chapter 37

Jeff

I should have known something was wrong. It was weird that the coaches kept looking at Scooter when they talked. At the time I just thought they were trying to figure out what was wrong with him.

He was definitely acting odd too. The drive home was four hours long, and he didn't say one word the whole time.

The least he could have done was tell me what happened.

Instead I had to find out about it two days later from Coach Doublas.

Scooter

I should have talked to Jeff about the scholarship. I know that.

I talked with my mom. She was so happy, she began sobbing.

I talked with Coach Douglas. He was surprised, of course, and angry at the way the situation was handled. But he was also impressed, I think. "Maybe you're more than a raw talent," he said. "If there's one thing Huntington's known for, it's great running backs."

I was going to ask both of them whether I should take the scholarship, but I didn't need to. They assumed I was going to take it, which means for them it was a no-brainer. No one in their right mind would turn down free college, would they?

So a day after Jeff's college visit (which turned out to be my college visit), I called Coach Grand and accepted his offer.

I know it was the right decision—the only logical decision, really.

But I still should have told Jeff before I made it.

Chapter 39

Jeff

After practice, the three of us were in Coach Douglas's office again.

Coach wanted to switch up the strategy.

"River Valley's defense is based on speed and blitzing," he said. "Which is why I want to try running this week out of the I formation."

"Coach?" I asked.

"A halfback." He looked at me carefully. "And a fullback. Look, Stoddard, I know this isn't the normal plan, but I really think it would help—just this week—if you were the lead blocker instead."

"Sure, Coach," I said.

"Really?"

"Sure," I said again. "Whatever the team needs."

It was easy to be a good teammate because, as far as I knew, I had a scholarship in the bag.

"In that case," Coach said, "we can talk more about this tomorrow at practice. You're dismissed."

We both got up to leave, but Coach stopped me. "Actually, Stoddard, could you stick around for a second?"

I sat back down while Scooter left the room.

"I just want to say that I'm impressed, Stoddard."

"Really, Coach, it's nothing."

"No—it's definitely something. You must have been really disappointed when you found out Huntington sold you a bad bill of goods, but here you are—"

"What are you talking about, Coach?"

Coach squinted at me. "You mean, they didn't tell you . . ." He rubbed his face, then slapped his desk. "This is ridiculous," he grumbled.

"Coach?" I said again. "What are you talking about?"

By now I was getting scared.

"The scholarship, Stoddard."

"What about it?"

"They gave it to Williams. I'm so sorry you had to find out this way. They had no right to leave you high and dry like that."

He kept talking, but I couldn't hear him anymore.

My pulse was beating too loudly in my ears. I needed to get out of there.

I needed to get out of *here*. Coach's office. The school. The town itself.

Scooter

After the meeting in Coach's office, I found my mom waiting for me in the parking lot. She was going to take me to dinner to celebrate the scholarship.

At least that was the plan.

The problem was, I didn't feel like celebrating. Not after that meeting.

Either Jeff was being amazingly cool about losing his last shot at a scholarship, or he still thought he was getting the scholarship. That would explain why he was in such a good mood. The thought made me feel sick.

I tried to remind myself that it wasn't like I'd stolen the scholarship. Coach Grand was clear that if I didn't take scholarship, he'd give it to someone else. Someone not named Jeff Stoddard.

But I still felt guilty. If the scout had never seen me play, maybe he would have been more impressed with Jeff. Maybe he didn't look fast enough because Eric was comparing him to me.

Mainly, I felt tired.

Tired of thinking about this scholarship and tired of football.

I definitely didn't want to talk about them.

Or anything, for that matter.

"I don't want to go to dinner, Mom."

We were on the road by then. She asked me what I *did* want to do.

"Can you drop me off somewhere?"

***

Splash!

It turned out I wasn't very good at skipping rocks. I was at Morgyn's pond, but Morgyn wasn't there. I crouched down and picked up another rock. Stepping into it, I chucked the stone toward the water.

Instead of skimming along its surface, it *splooshed* into the water and quickly sank.

I'd been here for at least twenty minutes, but I didn't feel better like I'd hoped I would. It's difficult to feel better when you stink at the thing you're using as a distraction.

I crouched down again and reached for another rock.

"Try this one," a voice said.

Morgyn was standing behind me. How long had she been there?

"Is it a good skipping rock?" I asked. "If it is, you should probably keep it. I don't want to screw up *your* favorite thing too."

I thought she was going to ask me what I was talking about, but she didn't.

"It's just one rock," she said. "The only way you could screw up rock skipping for me is if you got rid of every rock and drained the pond."

She held out the rock. I took it.

"The key to rock skipping," she said, "is the release. If the rock spins out of your hand the right way, the water doesn't even have to be calm. You should know whether the rock's going to skip without even having to watch."

Morgyn amazed me.

"Close your eyes," she said.

I did.

I threw the rock and we both listened to it *ping* across the water.

Jeff

I drove around for a while by myself. I wasn't ready to see anyone yet—not even Morgyn.

I was close to her house though, turning onto one dirt road after another, probably too fast. Dirt billowed behind the car.

I lost control of the car briefly and came swerving to a stop.

My heart pounded. I took a deep breath.

I was still a few blocks from Morgyn's house, but I decided to get out of my car and walk.

The dust my tires had kicked up was still settling as I worked my way through the woods and behind the house.

I found them there, at the pond, skipping stones together.

It was getting dark, but they were still clearly visible. It wasn't as though there was any question who the guy was. His tiny frame gave him away.

They were standing close to each other, taking turns.

One of them threw a stone and then they both leaned toward the pond, listening to sounds only they could hear—as if they shared some kind of secret.

I don't know how long I stood there, exactly.

Long enough to decide their secret wasn't safe with me.

Scooter

When I got to school the next morning, it was clear that something was different. For the last few weeks I hadn't been able to walk down the hall without getting a friendly clap on the shoulder. But today something was definitely wrong.

A few guys bumped into me. Most just steered clear of me.

I wondered if I was imagining things until the comments started.

"His scholarship, man?"

"His *girlfriend*?"

"Seriously. What's the matter with you?"

These comments kept coming throughout the morning. It seemed pointless to defend myself. There was no way they'd believe me.

The only thing I could think to do was talk to the guy who was spreading the rumors.

***

"Jeff?" I said at lunch. "Can we talk?"

He was sitting with the rest of the team at one of the long tables in the cafeteria. He didn't bother turning around.

"Oh. So *now* you want to talk?" he said.

"Look, Jeff—"

"The kid who never says anything suddenly has a lot he needs to say?"

"It's not—"

"Not what I think?" Jeff interrupted. "Is that what you're about to tell me? I think I took you on my college visit and you ended up with my scholarship. I think you've been hanging out with Morgyn behind my back. That's what I think. Are you saying I'm wrong?"

He was clearly furious. I could hear it in his voice.

"No," I said. "I mean, sort of. I mean—"

"In that case, I sort of forgive you. But I mostly think you're a scumbag."

"Look. Can we—"

That's when a couple guys stood up from the table. One of them put his hand on my chest and pushed. "Haven't you done enough, man?" he said.

"I just need to clear this up with Jeff," I said.

"Time's up," said the other guy.

"This is stupid. If I just had a few minutes I could—What are you doing? Are you kidding me?"

What they were doing was picking me up. The two of them carried me out of the cafeteria like I was some little kid having a temper tantrum. They put me down in the middle of a hallway.

"It's probably best that you stay clear of the cafeteria today," Cordell said.

They both walked away.

"See you at the game tonight," Mike said.

I couldn't help thinking it sounded like a threat.

Jeff

So that's what happened.

That's how Scooter ruined my life. He stole every part of it. Football—my starting spot and scholarship. And my escape from football—Morgyn.

And that brings us to right now.

Game time.

We get the ball first. We line up in the I formation, just as I agreed to do. More specifically, I line up as fullback. I agreed to do that too.

But that was before.

Before Coach filled me in on Scooter's betrayal.

Before I witnessed his betrayal firsthand at Morgyn's.

So you can understand if blocking for Scooter isn't exactly high on my priority list right now. Since my teammates know what he did to me, I don't think it's high on their priority list either.

Chapter 44

Scooter

Joey hands me the ball, and I wait for Jeff to lead the way through the line.

The problem is that Jeff is waiting too.

He doesn't wait for long—but it's long enough.

Long enough to let the River Valley players cross the line of scrimmage.

I have no choice but to run to the sideline. Hopefully, Jerrod Lemon, our tackle, is able to hold his own against their defensive end. Otherwise, I have nowhere to go.

Jerrod hardly moves. He takes one step toward the end, but that's it.

Just like that, the River Valley end is in

the backfield—so close I can practically smell his breath.

I'm quick, but I'm not *that* quick. He collapses on top of me before I can make a single move.

No one helps me off the turf.

"Williams!" Coach yells. "Follow your blocks!"

What blocks? I wonder.

We line up again for another run play. River Valley blitzes a linebacker, and this time Jeff is there to block for me.

Sort of.

Jeff's the strongest person I know, but the linebacker plows him over. I'm standing right behind Jeff. When he falls over, so do I.

Basically, I just got tackled by my own teammate.

One of the guys grabs Jeff's arm and lifts him to his feet. Nobody does the same for me.

Coach Douglas calls for a pass play on third down. It's incomplete, so we need to punt.

On the sidelines, Coach tries to encourage us: "Stick with the plan, boys," he says to Jeff and me. "We'll wear them down eventually."

"Yes, Coach," Jeff says.

And he's not lying. I'm sure he *is* going to stick with the plan.

Just not the plan Coach is referring to.

Jeff's plan isn't to execute the I formation. It's to let me get creamed by the other team.

***

Several minutes later we have the ball again. The game is still scoreless. And my teammates are still refusing to block for me.

I could try to scramble. To make something out of nothing.

But Coach was clear that he wants me to run into the teeth of the defense.

Besides, even if I beat four or five guys, there would still be six or seven others breathing down my neck. No one, not even Barry Sanders, can play one versus eleven.

Still, I'm nervous. I'm so anxious to get the ball and run away from the defense that I move before the ball is snapped.

The refs blow the whistle.

"False start!" one of them calls.

The others move the ball back five yards.

"C'mon, Williams!" Coach yells. "Get your head in the game!" I get the ball on the next play and run past Jeff's non-existent block right into three River Valley players.

It's not the hit itself that hurts. It's the collective weight of their bodies.

Jeff

I don't know what to make of Scooter. Is he crazy?

Over and over, we let him get pummeled.

I don't know what I want him to do. Apologize? Beg for forgiveness? For protection?

Maybe I just want him to quit.

Not just football but school too.

Maybe I want him to run off the field and keep on running—all the way back to where he came from.

If he quits, I think, everything could go back to normal.

But he doesn't quit.

Small as he is, he keeps charging into the line. Keeps taking his punishment. Keeps getting back up.

The next time he's left lying crumpled on the field, I stand over him.

"What's wrong with you?" I yell. "Say something! Why won't you ever say anything?!"

He hops to his feet.

"You want me to say something?" he yells. "Is that all you want? Fine! Here's what I say to you. Let's switch!"

"What?"

"You and me. Let's switch places. You be the halfback, I'll be the fullback. That's what you want, isn't it?"

I've never heard him scream like this.

We're all in a huddle now, but Scooter isn't done talking. "Jeff and I are going to switch places," he announces.

"No, we're not," I say.

"Seriously," he says, "anyone else want me to take their position? Anyone want *my* position?" He looks around the huddle, daring someone to speak up. His head isn't drooping now. "No? Great. Fullback it is."

"You'll get killed, man," I say.

"I'm getting pretty beat up as it is," he says. "Besides, I can do a heck of a lot better job than you are."

"Fine," I say. "You want to get clobbered, go ahead. Just don't blame me, okay?"

"I've got a better idea," Scooter says. "Why don't you stop blaming me?"

We break the huddle.

Scooter steps in front of me, gets in a crouch. Out of the corner of my eye I see Coach putting his hands together to signal a time out. I hear him start to yell, "Time—"

But he's too late. Joey yells, "Hut!" He takes the snap, pivots, gives me the ball. Scooter finds the guy who's blitzing and launches himself at him.

He's got courage—I'll give him that.

Unfortunately, Scooter's too small to make much of difference. The linebacker shrugs him off and then lowers his shoulder into me.

His shoulder pad connects full force with

my stomach, knocking the wind out of me. I stagger and fall.

Scooter and I lie next to each other on the field.

"He said he wouldn't have offered you the scholarship," Scooter says, in his usual soft voice.

"What?"

"The coach at Huntington." Scooter continues, this time with more urgency. "He said if I didn't take the scholarship he would find someone on a different team. He said he wasn't considering you. I'm sorry, Jeff. I should have said something. But I didn't know how to tell you. And I needed the scholarship. Without the money I won't be able to go to college at all."

I'm stunned. Should Scooter have told me about the scholarship? Absolutely. He should have told me a lot of things. If I'd known that he needed that scholarship to go to college, well, that would have helped too. Why *didn't* he tell me? Then again, why didn't I tell *him*? He had no idea how desperate I was for that scholarship. I've been so focused on *my* game, *my* future, *my* relationship with Morgyn— mine, mine, mine."

"Do you still blame me?" he finally asks.

"A little," I admit. "Do you still think I'm a jerk?"

"A little," he says.

"Then I guess we're even," I say.

We help each other up.

Scooter

"What *I* don't understand," Morgyn says to Jeff, "is why everyone thought I was your girlfriend."

The three of us are in her backyard, building a bonfire. All of Morgyn's friends are coming over soon, and some of the guys from the team might even stop by.

"They came up with that a long time ago," Jeff says. "At first it was a joke, and then I guess people started believing it."

"And you never corrected them?" Morgyn shakes her head. "Real mature of you."

Jeff looks embarrassed now. "Yeah,

sorry—it's not like I *said* you were my girlfriend. I just kind of let people draw their own conclusions. It was easier than telling them I was going to go hang out with some weird girl and skip rocks in the dark."

"Weird girl?" she says.

"I mean that as a compliment," he says. "I dig weird people."

He's kneeling, balancing some pieces of wood together.

"Take Scooter here. He's either weirdly quiet or weirdly loud." He laughs. "You should have seen him today on the field. The dude was freaking out."

"Seems like it worked," she says. "You guys were unstoppable in the second half."

Jeff and I look at her, surprised.

"You were at the game?" I ask.

"I go to all of your games," she says.

For a second Jeff looks stunned. "Wait, so you actually do care about football?"

She shrugs. "It's fun to watch sometimes."

"Did you ever consider telling us that?" Jeff asks.

"I don't know. Did you ever consider telling people that I'm not actually your girlfriend?"

"Okay—you're right. I'll make sure I straighten that out. But seriously, you're kind of blowing my mind. This is a whole side of you I didn't know about."

She raises her eyebrows. "I bet I have lots of sides you don't know about."

Jeff laughs again. "Well, like I said, you're both weirdos. It's a good thing I'm so normal. It keeps us balanced. Normal, abnormal. It's a yin and yang thing."

Or Thunder and Lightning, I think.

A few minutes later we have a nice fire going.

"Do you think the coaches at Huntington would let me walk on?" Jeff asks.

"Sure," I say. "Why not?"

"Don't look so happy about it," he says. "I'm coming after your job, man."

We're both smiling.

"Seems fair to me," I say.

About the Author

Paul Hoblin lives, teaches, and writes in Saint Paul, Minnesota.